Walter Savage Ball

Amherst Life

Walter Savage Ball

Amherst Life

ISBN/EAN: 9783337277161

Printed in Europe, USA, Canada, Australia, Japan

Cover: Foto ©Andreas Hilbeck / pixelio.de

More available books at **www.hansebooks.com**

AMHERST LIFE

Selections from the undergraduate publications at Am-
herst College : : :
Edited by Walter
Savage Ball : : :
Illustrated by W. ll-
iam Cary Duncan

Published by
WILLIAM CARPENTER HOWLAND
Amherst, mdcccxcvi.

PREFACE.

THE selections that make up this book
have been chosen from the various publications of the college in an endeavor to present, as faithfully as may be, a picture of
the real student life at Amherst; life being
best defined by the sophomore as "What
we talk about after dinner." In order to
accomplish this, mere literary excellence
has not been sought for, since this is but
one result of a single phase of college life.
Undergraduates will care more to remember what they talked about than how their
classmates wrote ; while those who have
already passed commencement day and the
parchment "rite" will at best think of
little merit the cleverness of undergraduate
style, but care much to feel again the student abandon, which once enabled them to
poke fun at the most sacred of their institutions or to moralize happily on the gravest
questions of their college life.

Of the three college publications, "The

Olio" contains by far the most of the typi-
cal student spirit.   In the more dignified
publications the college writer too often
leaves the rich and attractive field of undergraduate experiences to attempt the por-
trayal of scenes less familiar to himself and
less interesting to his readers.   "The Olio"
is at present almost the only place where the
familiar scenes of Amherst are dealt with.
Its position as the annual jest-book of the
college gives it a freedom of thought and
expression which, while they would often
be entirely out of place in either of the
other publications, nevertheless present
student ideas on the faculty, the town,
college customs and institutions, as found
nowhere else save in the student's private
den, amid clouds of laugh-tossed smoke.
These are the things that are remembered
in after years, and these are the things the
present book endeavors to preserve.

Several sketches which give expression
to the free views and critical observation
that characterize the student in his dealings
with his immediate surroundings have been
taken from the recent numbers of the
"Amherst Literary Monthly."   A few of
the best stories that have appeared in the

same magazine, describing Amherst scenes and illustrating the special features of Amherst life, are included.

The aim has been to make this distinctively an Amherst book. In accordance with this aim, a department has been given to articles on the Amherst senate, whose rise was viewed with so much interest by the colleges of the country and whose fall was mourned by the many friends of Amherst. Here will be found a letter written by an alumnus to the Amherst Student, at the time when the senate question was in special debate. In the same department are placed the undergraduate ideas on compulsory church and chapel. The lightly expressed sentiments of the student often convey in the directest manner his more earnest and thoughtful opinions on such questions as these. A book on Amherst life would also be incomplete to alumni, present and future, without some memories of the faculty, for many of the student's best ideas come in connection with the professor himself, rather than the professor's teaching, where they of course belong.

Aside from classing the selections under

the few very general topics the order of
arrangement has been left pretty much to
itself, thus illustrating the apparent irrel-
evancy of the experiences and thoughts of
him who has been called "the man with a
purpose alterable only by a dispensation of
Providence or a joke on his superiors":
the college undergraduate.

The selections in this book have been taken from the following sources:

From the Eighty-five Olio: "The Marking System," "Amherst Fire Department."

From the Eighty-six Olio: "A Short History of Amherst College."

From the Eighty-seven Olio : "Amherst Miscellany."

From the Eighty-eight Olio: "History of the Senate," "The Annual Picture Rush."

From the Eighty-nine Olio: "Dedication to the Senate."

From the Ninety-one Olio: "The Old Dormitories," "Ubi Sunt, O Pocula!"

From the Ninety-two Olio : "Extracts from the Catalogue," "To Julius Hawley Seelye," "Rime of the Ancient Derwall," "Compulsory Chapel Attendance."

From the Ninety-three Olio: "Chimes from the Dumb Bells," "The Convents."

From the Ninety-four Olio : "The Purple and White," "To Richie," "A Matin Idyl," "To the Pharisee."

CONTENTS.

xi

THE PURPLE AND WHITE.

Old Amherst, our loved Alma Mater,
 Enthroned on thy beautiful hill,
Thou fountain from whence purest water,
 In clear limpid streams does distill;
Thy symbols, the book and the sun,
 Shall together the far lands enlight.
All hail to thy glorious colors !
 Three cheers for the purple and white !

Fond memories of thee shall e'er linger,
 Enshrined in each son's loyal heart.
Thy precepts shall be as a finger,
 Directing our course on life's chart.
Thy name shall sound forth as our watchword,
 Leading into the thick of the fight,
As we press ever onward and upward,
 Proudly wearing the purple and white.

Rich purple, the old regal color,
 The badge now of thy royalty—
May its bright luster never grow duller—
 Ever strong as our own loyalty.
Together, with its fair companion,
 So pure, unspotted, and bright,
May it ever wave gloriously o'er us,
 Three cheers for the purple and white !

THE COLLEGE.

AMHERST LIFE.

A SHORT HISTORY OF AMHERST COLLEGE.

TO 1885.

(The writer of this history desires to express his obligations to Professor W. S. Tyler, from whose excellent history of Amherst College he has derived much information ; and also to Professor Genung and Lord Macaulay, whose styles he has tried to follow.)

THE want of a college in the Connecticut valley seems to have been felt previous to the Revolution, probably wanted by the starving storekeepers, and as there was a mother in Amherst for the college, it was established here some time after the want was felt.

The great natural beauty of the place had, perhaps, something to do with the

2

college being located in Amherst. On the east was Pelham, a great and flourishing metropolis, as large, if not larger, then than now, and there were the "Pelham daisies." The country about the north raised grapes and watermelons in abundance, and this could teach the students to look out for themselves. On the south there was a river, and that is all there is there now. On the west was Old Hadley, the Connecticut river, and Northampton. Students of the present day wonder what Hamp could have been in those days. Where were Smith and Miss Burnham's, and what would Hamp be without them? You can borrow a dollar there now.

But we were speaking of the founding of the college. There had been an effort to unite the mother to Williams, which was then a much larger and more flourishing college than it is now, but this finally fell through, as the Williams men wanted the earth. They don't now. But finally things came to a focus, and with the help of a Williams brother (how much we owe to Williams— they now teach us to play baseball!) and some masons the corner stone was laid August 9, 1820. We have tried to find it, but could not. It has probably gone to find the Starr Grove mines—another Amherst industry.

The college started in 1821, with Zephaniah Swift Moore of Williams (Williams again) as president. We will here remark that Williams seems to be as much the mother of Amherst College, as the Amherst Academy, and we are compelled in acknowledging the relationship to quote from Horace : *O matre pulchra filia pulchrior.*

The college was first called, and was, perhaps, a charity institution. We merely make this allusion to show how things change. No one would call it a charity institution now. There is no charity shown to students, or there would be no afternoon service on Sundays, and the editors of this publication would receive good scholarships, but we may get them yet.

The term bills were $10 and $11, and the students received as much instruction as we do now for $50, but they could not attend prayers and church as often. So we pay $88 per year for religious services—but we get our money's worth.

Board was from $1 to $1.25 per week, and with the faculty grapes and Sunderland watermelons, the students probably had enough to eat.

From its foundation up to February 21, 1825, the college got along without a charter, but on that date one was granted, and Amherst became one of the chartered colleges of the land. How many of the faculty and students have ever seen this charter ?

In August, 1830, a great event occurred, namely, the founding of the Antivenenean society. The members swore off on about everything except watermelons and chapel, and the society was, and is now, one of the most popular in college. There have also been missionary bands in the college. The early bands converted the heathen in Pelham and Hadley, and the one now in college is trying to convert the members themselves.

The college has received in all but $52,-500 from the state, not a third of what a small college at Williamstown, or not a tithe of what Harvard has received, but has always looked out and cared for herself.

The college has funds amounting to $595,000 (or had some years ago; it is probably larger now). The value of the buildings, funds, etc., is over a million dollars, and yet we are burdened twice a year by a note reading as follows :

Amherst College, ...

Mr. . . . . ,

DEAR SIR :

The first (or second) installment of your term bill is still unpaid. Please give it your prompt attention.

Yours truly,

W. A. DICKINSON,

Treasurer.

Comment is unnecessary.

As tall oaks from little acorns grow, our college has grown so that now its branches cover many lands, while its roots derive nourishment from every country and every clime. Amherst has brave men in foreign lands working for the gospel of Christ. She has given lawmakers to our country, and has sent forth some of the greatest preachers of modern times. She has never given a president of the United States, or a pickpocket, but many of us are young yet.

All old and young graduates love Amherst, and when we go forth to our labors, among the happiest of our memories will be the days of our college life. When far away we can see as though in a dream, the rushes, rope-pulls, and rackets; the cutting, cribbing, and convents; the ball games and athletics; and we can also hear the college yell, and can almost see, rising and floating above all, the purple and white of old Amherst.

So while we sit and muse these words will come to us:

> " And eastward still, upon the last green step,
> From which the angel of the morning light
> Leaps to the meadow lands, fair Amherst sat,
> Capped by her many-windowed colleges."

And, while in the midst of these recollections we are

> " Kind o' smily round the lips,
> And teary round the lashes,"

we will say down deep in our hearts: "God bless and keep old Amherst!"

EXTRACTS FROM THE CATA-
LOGUE.

ADMINISTRATION.

The following are the principles of ad-
ministration observed :

(1.) Work is assigned the student with
careful reference to his capacity. This is
especially true in the section of modern
languages; this section points with pride to
the fact that out of 976 students who have
taken German or Italian 6½ years, only ½
per cent. have died from brain fever, and
in his case it was sunstroke.

(2.) The student should make the utmost
improvement of his time and talents in
regularly and diligently doing what the
athletic association assigns him.

(3.) No student should be continued in a
class for which he is unfit; no man who
cannot horse accurately and fluently need
apply for any monitorship.

(4.) Every student is expected to cut one-
tenth of all his recitations, or his case will
come up before the senate.

(5.) Regularity of attendance on the

religious services is required, but close attention is purely optional. The section of English literature will on application furnish lists of good books for use in connection with these services.

THE PORTER ADMISSION PRIZE.

Any freshman who takes this prize is expected to loaf, get fired out of Pott's, and suffer from swelled head.

MATHEMATICS.

The instruction during freshman year is devoted to geometry, algebra, and trigonometry. In addition, the advanced division during the spring term pursues a course of surveying under the auspices of the athletic association.

HYGIENE.

The freshmen are first instructed in the use of the various parts of the student body, and this is followed by laboratory work in the gymnasium. In the spring term a slight amount of study in human physiology is allowed, supplemented by many anatomical preparations and amusing illustrations. All students are required to take this course, and very few ever regret it.

EXPENSES.

Term bills......................	$110.00
Room rent......................	2.00
Fuel (in dormitories) and lights...	45.00
Board (Merrick's)...............	13.50
Doctor's bills (Merrick's).........	60.00
Total......................	$230.50

A higher rent is charged for some of the best rooms in the dormitories and in town. Expenses vary according to the character and luxurious habits of the students. They can be materially reduced by borrowing kerosene and stealing coal.

HALLOCK PARK.

This is an original forest of six acres, to which the attention of the sporting fraternity is now directed. It is well stocked with canaries and other game birds. Some of the trees have been measured with a theodolite, and they are 30 feet 6½ inches high. Only a little underbrush has been left; a wagon road for the use of heavy teams passes through it, and lovers of the beautiful are allowed without extra charge to watch the trains on the Central Massachusetts get stuck in the cut, or gaze at the fences on the other side of the cut or around Blake field. The park is very near Pratt field, and can be easily reached from there by way of Pelham. Students generally frequent this lovely spot in moments of leisure, or for the enjoyment of its facilities for quiet study.

A. P. A.

AMHERST PICKPOCKET ASSOCIATION.
FOUNDED IN 1821.

Object—By a closer fraternal union of the members to promote their mutual interests.

History—Started by the townspeople in 1821, it has been virtually under their control ever since. All are members, from the young imp old enough to run errands, to the venerable retired minister of the gospel, who, all aglow with kindliness and benevolence, labors to convince the anxious parent of the immense advantage that his son will receive in having a gray-haired guardian and adviser who can guide the inexperienced youth safely through (?) the many snares

and pitfalls of college life, particularly of
freshman year.

The proceedings of the Association have
always been characterized by the greatest
unanimity and singleness of aim, and until
recently no signs of internal dissension
have been perceived.

The first meeting of the year was held
early in the opening week of fall term, and
at first promised to be no more eventful
than usual. After initiating the latest addi-
tions to the faculty, and granting the degree
of E. P. (Eminent Purloiner) to two tutors
for their zealous work in behalf of the association in their respective departments, the
society proceeded to business. The report
of the committee appointed at the last
meeting to procure designs for badges was
called for, and after much discussion a bit
of sponge tied to the buttonhole with a
gilt ribbon was adopted, as being most appropriate. The salute was also changed.
Formerly it had been given by laying the
forefinger of the right hand along the nose,
and winking with the left eye. Now it was
to be made by placing the hand with three
fingers extended, upon the right breast
pocket of the coat, that being the pocket

where the members supposedly carried
their pocketbooks.   Tip objected on the
ground that he carried his in his hat, and a
special exception was made in his case.

Next, secretary Swamp read his annual
report.   He said that the society was not
as strong in some points as it should be,
and care should be taken not to kill the
goose that was laying the golden egg.   The
"co-op" store showed a falling off in its returns.   The lecture course had kicked the
bucket.   The new "lab" with its unright-
eous fees, was a winning card, but in order
to silence the murmurs of the victims, the
association had been obliged to give up
vespers, and it looked now, as if compul—
er—institutional worship would have to go
too.   At this, Spear's representative arose
and objected so strenuously on the ground
that it would ruin the trade in novels, that
the idea was abandoned at once.   Then
Swampy suggested that "gym" drill be sac-
rificed, but at that Old Doc leaped to his
feet.   It wouldn't do.   The Hitchcock and
Blodgett syndicate had been by far the
most productive scheme yet put in practice,
and he wasn't going to see it pinched, not
by a good deal.   It was bad enough as it

was. There had long been a demand for sweaters in place of the useless blue bags that Blodgett furnished as coats, and now Ninety-seven had gone and worn tennis trousers at the Lincoln exhibition. Prexy here rapped for order, and suggested that they let the matter rest until he had thrown out a few more sops from the chapel pulpit. He could tickle the boys a little on athletics, scholarship, good-behavior, and so on. They could even bring up the senate matter again. It wouldn't do any harm to talk about it, and it might pacify the victims for a while. He guessed that with a little oil things would move on pretty smoothly.

The advisability of establishing branch associations at Hamp and Springfield was next discussed, but it was finally decided to be unnecessary.

The meeting was then adjourned, and the members repaired to Brother Deuel's, where they partook of ——— on the new initiates.

AS TO COLLEGE HALL.

THERE has been considerable discussion
of late among archæologists in regard to
the origin and identity of college hall. Professor Sterret had at one time actually
made up his mind to discover in it the sites
of Lystra and Derbe, but wisely changed
his mind at the last moment, and chose the
far East instead, on account of its more
healthful climate.

The Noah's ark theory is another popular fancy in relation to our relic of pre-
historic architecture situated next the
library. Professor Elwell says that "the
building corresponds most decidedly with
the recollections which he has of that historic craft." The fact that good, respect-
able doves can be induced to take up their
abode in the ramshackle tower, points
strongly to some deep-seated cause for
their affection other than any passing fancy.
The professor even claims that he has seen
the swift birds winging their way toward
the tower with olive branches in their
mouths, but on closer questioning it was

found to have occurred in the nesting season, and the so-called olive branches were
proven to be straws from a stable-yard.
Professor Frink claims that the west end of
the building, at least, is a part of the
original garden of Eden, for he says it
always seems like paradise to him. His
protégés, on the other hand, are unanimous
in the opinion that it is the famous "Black
Hole of Calcutta," renovated and restored,
but possessing, nevertheless, many of the
features of the original.

Trembling undergraduates at examination time have hinted that it was the well-
known "lion's den" of Bible story, and
between chattering teeth have sung "Dare
to be a Daniel," as they entered its awful
portals.

The Amherst G. A. R., with character-
istic originality, positively asserted that it
was Libby Prison, until Libby Prisons became as common at all large expositions as
pieces of the true cross in Old World mon-
asteries; and the idea was abandoned as
too commonplace.

A dispute then arose on the question of
choice between the battleship *Merrimac*
and the house where Lee surrendered, a

compromise being finally effected and Fort
Sumter chosen as the lucky place. These
are but a few of the latest nineteenth-cen-
tury suggestions as to college hall. All
differ widely and all have some plausible
points. THE OLIO cannot and cares not to
discriminate. All it claims is that the old
wreck ought to be put under glass and
preserved for what it is—a relic; not forced
into unseemly use as a hall of learning.
People do not use Indian arrow heads for
cobble stones, nor the "true cross" to
train pea vines on. There is a propriety
which demands that college hall be laid on
the shelf or torn down.

THE OLD DORMITORIES (1890).

AMONG the many superior advantages
which our college affords, none are more
noteworthy than those which are offered by
a residence in one of our admirable dormitories. The dormitory system is so
simple and so complete, that to mention it
in other terms than those of the highest

praise would be to betray a carping spirit indeed. Perhaps the most elegant of them all is that known as North Purgatory. This building exhibits all of the Greek simplicity, but abhors those ultra refinements which, we are told, finally resulted·in the spinal curvature of Greek outlines in general. Within are spacious rooms, which are arranged with great economy of space, being hampered by none of those obstructing angles and shelving roofs which abound in buildings of the hybrid "Queen Anne" order. The hall-ways are provided with board floors, and there are three flights of stairs for the convenience of the students. Hardly less handsome and commodious, and an almost equal favorite, is the dormitory known as South Sheol. On the fourth floor of this building are the favorite rooms, looking out upon the tennis court and that beautiful specimen of modern architecture, the Appleton cabinet. The facilities for exercise afforded by these apartments are excellent, as coal may be carried from the basement up the three flights of stairs at the will of the student. The social advantages secured by a life in these noble dormitories are too well known to need

3

enumeration here. Enough to say that
these advantages are unsurpassed by those
of any lunatic asylum in the country, and
that the character of their occupants is in
keeping with the incomparable tone of the
buildings themselves.

TO THE TRUSTEES,

OR whoever is responsible for the selec-
tion of the site of the new laboratory, we
tender our most hearty congratulations.
For inconvenience of access and general
unsightliness it certainly surpasses any
other location in town. It is difficult to
imagine what deterred those controlling
the location of the building from placing it
on the Pelham hills. There it would have
been a landmark visible for miles in all
directions. All possibility of its being
regarded as a part of the gas works or hat
shops would thus have been avoided, and
as for convenience—well, that doesn't appear to cut any figure in the consideration.
    It is to be hoped that Pete, Amherst's

only ticket speculator, or some other phil-
anthropic "sharper," ever mindful of the
student's interests, will at once inaugu-
rate a stage line to run between the various fraternity houses and our suburban
laboratory.

FACULTY AND COURSES.

TO JULIUS HAWLEY SEELYE.
(1891.)

In the twilight of life, when the husbandman's labor is done,
Let him rest from the cares of the day, who
hath labored so well 'neath the sun.
For his service was honest and good since
his service began,
As becometh a worker in truth who is toil-
ing for God and for man.
In the autumn of life, when the husbandman, weary and gray,
Findeth rest from his summer of toil, let
our honor his labor repay.
Let him rest as the husbandman rests, with
his loved and his own,
While he leaveth to others the fruit of the
seed that his spirit hath sown.
For the russet or gold of his harvest already
appears,
And the reapers are stalwart and young
who shall garner the wealth of his
years ;

And their hands shall be willing and glad,
and their spirit be strong,
As they harvest the fruit of his toil, and
remember his worth in a song.

———

TWO VERSES.

IN MEMORIAM JULIUS H. SEELYE, 1895.

I.

A BIRD sang sweet and loud,—
He kissed a little child:
A rainbow burst a cloud,—
He took a sinner's hand:
A fruit tree blossomed white,—
A death sting he beguiled:
A blind man found his sight,—
He made him understand.

II.

He towered head and shoulders over aver-
age man,
A noble figure that yet blessed the land
it trod;
I said, he stands upright as only godlike can,
I said, his head is high because he talks
with God

A GENERAL ESTIMATE.

EXTRACT FROM A PAMPHLET DISCOVERED IN 4000 A. D.

AND in a certain place named Massachusetts there was founded, in 1821, a college called Amherst. It has not yet been ascertained whether the College derived its name from the town in which it was situated, but beyond a doubt it was the most noted of all similar institutions on account of the quaint and peculiar body of men which in those days was known as the faculty. Many nice young men came to this place in the fall, and stayed until the following summer. It is supposed that they came here to instruct the faculty concerning the movements of the world outside of Amherst. The so-called faculty were not " up " in this particular branch. No blame is attached to them, however, on this account, because they had belonged to the College for so long a time and had been handed down from epoch to epoch, generation after generation, that the institution

felt bound to hold them in restraint, lest
some more formidable body like Fore-
paugh's circus or Dartmouth College might
capture and make way with them.

TO "GOOD OLD DOC."

OUR Good Old Doc's a man,
 A man who needs no praise;
To whom be peace and honor,
 Sound health and length of days.

With step that's firm and quick,
 With accents sharp and true,
With way that's bright and cheery,
 In truth—a man for you.

No student has a friend
 Who'll aid near half as well,
Or last so long and faithful
 As Doc, of whom we tell.

And when in after years
 We all come back again,
We'll greet Doc then right royal
 With voice and not with pen.

For Good Old Doc's a man,
  A man right through and through,
And though his locks are silver,
  He's young as I—or you.

And so let honor rest
  Upon that silver head,
And peace with gentle motion
  Her golden wings outspread.

For Good Old Doc's a man,
  A man right through and through,
And though his locks are silver,
  He's young as I—or you.

———

PROFESSOR GARMAN.

A MAN whom Wisdom's children long
To know; and knowing come to trust;
And trusting learn to love.   He strikes
The deepest, noblest chords within
Our hearts, and teaches us to know
Ourselves, our fellows, and our God.

From Tips' biological lectures : "If I should ever preach in the college church,— if such a thing were conceivable,—I would preach on the Sabbath ; and I don't know as I should say very much about the Sabbath either. I would emphasize the other part of the text : 'Six days shalt thou labor.'"

TO THE HEAD OF THE GERMAN DEPARTMENT.

If you're fond of racy stories,
    If you want a spicy joke,
If you like to hear related
    A pleasant anecdote ;
If your quest is for a teacher
    Who will never be a bore,
Then hie you to the portals wide
    Of Richie's class-room door.

If what you want is wisdom,
    Well mixed with common sense,
If you wish to hear life's problems
    Discussed with eloquence,

If you like a plain and earnest man,
Who's a man right through and through,
Then Richie is the proper one
To fill the bill for you.

———

OUR MARKING SYSTEM.

THE FACULTY SLIP.

Mr. X.—

Latin, ...	3⅞
Greek, ...	3⅝
Mathematics, . . .	4½

3 | 12

Actual mark, ... 4

THE STUDENT SLIP.

Mr. X.—

Latin, ...	3
Greek, ...	3
Mathematics, ...	4

3 | 10

Your mark for last term was . . 3

E. B. MARSH.

CHIMES FROM THE DUMB-BELLS.

"Gentlemen! By—by my eternal birth-right, if I see another one of you throw-ing a dumb-bell across this floor, I will hand him over to the captain for fifty cents a dumb-bell. You may think that it's smart, and funny, but it isn't. I know you're young and green yet, and feel good and like to frisk round and let yourselves loose now and then like new-born calves, but, gentlemen, I *do* draw the line some-where. I don't very often say, 'you shall,' and 'you sha'n't!' but there are some things which must be held sacred even in this gymnasium. You know they have a day in the church calendar which they call 'All Saints' Day'; now I think that you're like the church. You have the day, but I'd like to name it 'All Devils' Day.' [Long continued yells and stamping.] *Gentlemen!* Gentlemen! I command you to atten-tion. [Silence after a while.] When my father heard that I was to have charge of the gymnasium, says he, 'Edward, my son, you'll have to be pretty free with the boys and take care not to put too tight a restraint upon them,' and I've found out that it's so. It's always best to be obliging to you *young* men, but I'll have you to understand that my powers of endurance have a limit. I can dismiss the class; I never had to do such a thing before, but if I see any more such monkey-shines as you've indulged in this morning, I vow I'll do it."

"All right, I believe, Mr. Captain."

N. B.—We might remark that after this speech an event happened which had never taken place before in the history of Amherst college. "Old Doc," actually forgot to say, "Gentlemen, the men marked absent are," etc.

RICHIE's jokes are pungent quite,
Sometimes, mayhap, rather trite;
Richie is a "merry wight,"
And his marks are out of sight.

STUDENT (making out report in the Physics Laboratory)—Well, hang it, what was the object of this experiment, anyhow?

VOICE (from a fellow slave)—To get back your $3 lab. fee.

RICHIE has some pretty good ideas in his head. His latest, as expressed to his class, is—

" Work like thunder.
Play like thunder.
Rest like thunder.
Yes, by thunder ! "

———

THE RIME OF THE ANCIENT DERWALL.

I.

SOMEWHAT back from the college street
Stands the " lab."   Oh, sweet retreat !
Around its antique, weather-beaten door
The spirits of tortured sophomores loudly
    roar,
And from his station in the room
The ancient Derwall says to all who come,
" Five dollars more for Ned, for Ned;
    Five dollars more for Ned ! "

II.

Leaning halfway over the counter he stands,
And points and beckons with his hands.

Still he utters this solemn croak
(While the sophomore, under his cloak,
Pities himself and sighs, alas !
I'd give a fiver to be elected to pass),
"You must not think, not think,
    You must not think."

III.

By day his step is low and light,
But in the silent dead of night,
Distinct his passing footsteps fall;
They echo along the vacant hall—
Along the ceiling, along the floor
As he pauses at the bottle of H_2SO_4,
"Your process will stick 'em, will stick
        'em;
    Your process will stick 'em."

IV.

Through days of grind and days of mirth,
Through days of cuts and days of dearth,
Through every swift vicissitude
Of changeful time, unchanged he's stood.
And as if, forever, he all things saw,
He quietly sends these words of awe:
" Your mark is below two, 'low two;
    Your mark is below two."

4

V.

Within that "lab" in festive glee,
Sports a tutor from the faculty.
Wild spirits round the laboratory roared,
While the "Faculty" counted their hoard.
But like the skeleton at the feast,
That warning Derwall never ceased,
    "Twenty-five I've stuck, I've stuck;
    Twenty-five I've stuck."

VI.

There groups of merry seniors played,
There fresh and juniors carefully strayed,
Oh, precious hours!   Oh, golden prime !
Sufficiency of money, "supe," and time.
E'en as a miser counts his gold,
These hours the young Doc carefully told.
    "You'll pass very soon, very soon;
    You'll pass very soon."

VII.

We will all be scattered soon, and fled;
Some in prison, some still under Ned.
When   found, to freshmen we   give this
        advice,
If you want a "gut," a "snap," something
        nice,

Elect "Derwall"; but as they hurry
    swiftly by,
The ghosts of former classes make reply :
"Yes; but not now, not now;
    Yes, but not now."

VISITOR (passing Walker hall, 2 P. M.)—
What is this noise I hear at the left ? The
boys cheering down at the football field ?
    STUDENT.—Oh, no ! That's the German
division laughing at one of Richie's jokes.

OLD DERWALL ON MEMORY.

Now, gentl'mun, er—right here, now, I'll
—er—make a few remarks, yer know, on—
er—on–er–r–r—mem'ry, yer know. Mem'ry
is a valuable thing if we—er—ta–ta—if er—
yer hev it, yer know, and don't fergit !
Now, you learn a lot o' things about this
and that and th' other, and you keep 'em
'bout a day, yer know, and—er–r–r–r–um–
er–r–um–eh ! eh ! eh ! and then, yer know
(here Derwall gets warmed up), and then—

a-a-a—yer fergit all-l-l 'bout um; yes, all
'bout um. Well now, gentl'mun, thet's not
the right way; mem'ry is ter remember
things by, yer know—a-and if—a—mm—a
yer fergit all you ever learn, yer'll never
know much. You must learn, gentl'mun,
to 'sociate one thing with another and—a-
a-mm-a-ta-a-ta-a—m-make an impression
on your mind, y' know, then you wunt
fergit.

Now, fer example, s'posin' two of you
fellers—er—were ridin' out in a kerrige,
well—er-a-er—say—ter—ter Hamp ! Yer
—a-talkin' 'bout this thing and that—and—
a-a lot of other nonsense, yer know !
Don't make much diff'rence, y' know, and
yer don't care whether it's raining up er
down ! Well now, yer know, 'sposin' yer
git onter the railroad crossin' between here
and Ha-adley, a—mm-a-er—and—er-r-r—
yer know, while yer a talkin' and a foolin',
ye' know, the car comes down the track-a,
and cleans yer horse right out from in front
of yer, what then ! Do yer fergit that
right off? N-o-o, sir ! a-a-nd if yer come
back to—a—yer A-a-lma Mater fifty years
afterward, yer know, and ride over to
Hamp, yer'll remember it just s'f 'twas

yisterday. A-a-and—er—yer know, it's because it made an impression on yer, and yer 'sociated every part of that ride—a—ta —a—on the a-accident, y' know. Well, now, gentl'mun, it's exactly the same way in chemistry, yer know, this—a–mm–a 'socią- tion of ideas and–a this making an impres- sion on yer minds.

Now–a, can someone tell me *quick*—a- mm-a-a—what's—a—the result if you pour water on—a phosph'rus (???) quick ! ! (And the recitation goes on as before.)

THE SENATE AND COMPULSORY CHURCH.

COMPULSORY CHAPEL ATTEND-
ANCE. ˙˙

THE tired Amherst student who recol-
lects the crusade in which THE STUDENT
embarked a year or two ago, may, when he
reaches this page of the "Olio," turn two
leaves at once and say "Rats !" The
remark would apply with much force, no
doubt, and especially to the thing itself.
The unvarying grind to which we become
so accustomed; scuttling up the hill, a
complaining beefsteak within; the race on
the stairs as the clock begins to strike; the
well-worn hymn; the same old prayer; the
monitors stretching their necks for the
absent, and the sneaking student who hides
his Potts or psych behind his neighbor's
back. They are all too familiar visions.

But the most familiar and significant
thing of all, as we review our short term of
college life, is the vivid emptiness of the
faculty seats. Day after day these leaders
of the blind present a noble array of five

good men and true, in representation of a total thirty! Day after day the farce is repeated; the morally stimulating lacteal nutriment is doled out to four hundred students who must swallow it, while a mere committee of the faculty attend to see the dose administered. The only variety is an occasional communication from the athletic moguls, said communication being limited to five minutes in length, a "Library Talk," unlimited, or the perennial dog with the handkerchief on his tail.

The attitude of our faculty on the subject is a fine illustration of the good old sophomore debate question : "Is the hope of reward a greater incentive to activity than the fear of punishment?" Indeed, we doubt that many, even of the most regular, attendants on chapel exercise have any idea to what extent the teachers, impelled to be present only by the hope of laying up treasure in heaven, cut the morning prayers. . . The view which every unprejudiced man will take is, no doubt, this : Our faculty look upon compulsory chapel as a convenience, a means of gathering the students together; a time for the reading of prayer-meeting and recitation notices, and *possibly*, to young men, a season of good influence; they consider personal example and attendance unnecessary; they come when they choose, they stay away because they may; and when we are free from the burden of extra work on account of extra absence, we will do the same.

A LIGHT VERSE DOXOLOGY.

FIENDS around us,
Fiends below,
All intent on
Bringing woe ;
Fiends on this earth
Do their work,
At compulsa-
Tory church.
Fill the kicker's
Mind with sin,
So that hell can
Take him in.
Thus God's house is
Blindly run,
So the devil's
Work is done.

SATIRES OF AMHERST.

BOOK I.—SATIRE I.

AWAKE, my Muse, get out thy sounding
   lyre,
And strike the chords that in our hearts
   inspire
The sense to know what's right and what is
   wrong;
Tune up, O Muse, and let's begin the song.
The evils which beset our paths are few,
Can be endured, excepting one or two;
But ye, immortal gods, who drain the cup
Of nectar, and upon ambrosia sup,
These evils are the kind that make men
   weep
And tear their hair and long for endless
   sleep,
On Martinique's fair isle, where kindly rays
From glistening Sol the ripe bananas raise,
(Steady, my Muse, such puns are not
   allowed;
Such low-born sporting frets your spirit
   proud),
Within the cluster, tempting to the eye
The serpent *fer de lance* doth lurking lie;

His yellow coils by luscious fruit con-
cealed
Are in no way unto the eye revealed.
But there he waits, the dreadful *fer de
lance,*
And let some hungry passer-by by chance-.
Reach forth his hand—a sudden hiss—a
cry—
A swiftly darting tongue—a gleaming
eye—
And 'neath the tree there lies the passer-
by.

"And why this story?" some of you may
say.
Give heed then while I tell you, if I may.
The ripe banana bunch doth represent
This seat of learning, where each year are
sent
To cull its choicest fruits, a band of
youth—
A chosen band—who search for higher
truth,
But Satan, like the hideous *fer de lance,*
Abideth here, and lurking waits his chance.
Religion here compulsory is made,
And thus the plot for Beelzebub is laid.
For worship to man's inner soul pertains;

If made compulsory it nothing gains,
But loses all, and its own end defeats
When with imperatives man's soul it meets.
Love wells spontaneous from the human
    heart,
And "must" and "shall" therein have not
    a part.
But to return—this chosen band of
    youth—
These earnest seekers after higher
    truth—
Set out to church, some filled with notions
    good,
And some coerced by fear of Swampy's
    rod.
And here the devil plays a winning hand,
For, like the snake in Martinique's fair
    land,
He fastens on the youths whose souls rebel
Against compulsory religion fell;
And some escape and some go do down
    to—well;
Our simile is ended; now we'll cease.
Go home, dear Muse, and rest and take thy
    ease.

THE SNAKE EDITOR'S DREAM.

IT was one warm spring day of sophomore year, one of those days which take a
man away from his lessons and carry him
back to the time when he was young and
sinless, and had yet to serve his time in
preparatory school and college. I was
leaning back in my chair with a half-smoked
cigarette in my teeth, and the blue coils of
smoke with their strange fantastic shapes
brought before my mind free and happy
boyhood days, where compulsory church
and Tip Ty were alike unknown, and where
the Westminster Shorter Catechism was
my only trial. Such thoughts were so hazy
and so indistinct that I rested my head
wearily against the wall and wept at the
changes which time had wrought.

As I leaned there in despair a film seemed
to come over my eyes, even such a film as
Paine's Celery Compound is guaranteed to
remove. The cigarette suddenly assumed
such colossal proportions that my cowed
and beaten spirit drew back in terror
against the wall. Then it began slowly to

change. Little by little arms, legs, and
a tail appeared, and in a moment there
stood before me a nicotine representative
of the devil. At last the truth burst upon
me. I was dreaming! For weeks and
months I had striven to dream. I had
eaten pickles and green fruit and washed
them down with the vilest of lager in the
vain hope that I might dream something
for the "Olio," but my toils had all been
in vain. I had even boarded at Merrick's
to accomplish my purpose, but it was of no
avail. And now, at last, when I had almost
given up the struggle, success had come.
I could scarcely conceal my joy. I felt
like grasping the specter by the hand and
thanking him for his welcome visit, when
he interrupted my joyful thoughts with
a solemn beckoning. Without uttering a
word I followed him. Soon we came to
the bank of a surging stream, where a for-
bidding-looking fisherman with dark hair
and beard was standing in his skiff ready
to ferry us across. When my companion
with the nicotine visage addressed him as
Mr. Charon, my heart leaped with joy.
Ha! ha! This was even better than I had
anticipated. I was going to visit the devil.

I would get a chance to interview him; to interview him for the "Olio"! In a short time we landed on the other bank and a mighty wind lifted us and bore us away. In time this wind carried us against a dark mountain, and before the wand of my strange guide the sides of the mountain opened and disclosed a wondrous country.

In silence I followed my companion, who walked briskly up to a brazen gate, dropped an obol in the slot, and a three-headed dog came forth wagging his tail with a sickening irregular motion that showed an utter lack of team work. Nimbly we sprang in. I had hardly entered when I tripped over the tail of an imp whom I afterward found to be quarter-back on the All-Hell football team. As I picked myself up and spit the brimstone out of my mouth, I said in broken tones to my companion: "Well, this *is* hell." "Of course," he replied; "you ought to have known that from Cerby." Amid the shrieks and groans of millions of people I was borne away to meet "His Satanic Tailship." "What have we here?" shouted the devil. "A student, most respectful joblots," humbly responded my guide. "A student! What does he want?" asked the

5

J

devil. "Is he dreaming?" "He is, Most
Potent Wearer of the Crooked Hoof,"
again replied my companion. "Ha! ha!
He dreams, does he? Answer me, young
man, answer me truly, are you intending to
write up this dream for publication?" For
a moment my courage forsook me. For a
moment I hovered between the right and
wrong, but only for a moment; then my train-
ing in swearing off cuts got in its fine work,
and I promptly answered "No." This satisfied the devil and he told me to step aside.

Hardly had I vacated my place when
Beelzebub, with the rest of the football
team, came in with a new corpse. As soon
as he had got within hearing distance,
Beelzebub shouted out at the top of his
voice: "A college professor!" The devil
actually went wild. He wrapped his cloven
hoof around his neck three times in a long,
loving embrace. Then he jumped down
from his throne and began to prepare the
skillet. "Throw him in!" he yelled.
"Roast him! Extract his fourth root!
Cut off the cologarithm of his cosine!
Season him with Jebbs and Potts! Grab
his femur, Beelzy, and run down the Mid-
way with it. Ha! ha! ha! This is fruit!

This is regular cantaloupe!" His frenzy was awful. Great beads of brimstone stood upon his brow, and his tail described un-plotable parabolic curves.

I hated to tarry in proximity to such a demon, yet I disliked to leave without securing my interview. As soon as the devil had recovered from his first wild paroxysms I plucked him by the sleeve. "Say, Satan, old girl, do you believe in compulsory church?"

"Believe in it!" he howled. "Believe in it! Why, young man, it's the only system. Who wants to abolish it but cranks and fools? I'll have nothing left by and by. They've done away with the fagot and the stocks, and they've succeeded in abolishing slavery, but I've got the saloon and compulsory church left, and I defy them to knock out either of them. Away with this opponent of compulsory church! Away with him, Cigaretto!" My companion grabbed me by the leg. His hand burned like fire, and I awoke to find my cigarette complacently burning a hole in my only pair of trousers.

[Let no Joseph endeavor to interpret this dream.]

HISTORY OF THE SENATE TO 1887.

SINCE the days of the renowned Dr. Thomas Arnold of Rugby, student self-government has been the Utopian dream of college presidents, of whom none more than President Seelye of Amherst saw the desirability of the system, and none sooner than he sought to put it into execution. About five years ago this cherished idea took definite form, when the body now known as the "Amherst College Senate" was organized, upon the same general plan which determines its existence to-day.

At first, the senate was of little or no use. It being an experiment, the president's policy was very conservative. He gave it no defined powers; he reserved the right to introduce all business; he retained the power of absolute veto. But little business was transacted. The usual proceedings were a speech from the President, congratulating himself and the senators that the present affairs of the college were in such an excellent condition as to require no legislation or adjudication, followed by adjournment. When any business was transacted, it was of such slight significance that it never reached the ear of the student body politic. The result of this tentative policy of the president was to bring the senate into disrepute. If spoken of at all, it was spoken of with a sneer or a jest. It was called "a farce," or "a cat's paw of the faculty," or some similar contemptuous epithet.

After three years of such existence, a sentiment was formed in college that the senate was of no use to the students, however valuable it might be to the faculty and the college president; that the senate must do something, or do away with the pretense of self-government.

In this crisis a constitution of defined power was demanded of the president. He was not disposed to grant it. He desired the constitution to form like the English constitution—by the precedence of its acts. The senators preferred the United States plan, thinking it better adapted to the circumstances. At length a constitution was obtained. It did not embody all that the senators desired, but it was, at least, a step out of non-existence into existence. However few and limited the powers obtained,

they were at least defined, and not subject
to variance by circumstance and arbitrary
will. The senate revived, became a much
more respected body, and entered on a
career that may end in usefulness. But it
is still a weakly institution. It has scarcely
enough power to give it a sufficient vitality
to live, much less to make itself felt in the
regulation of college affairs. It may have
all the power which at present can be given
it judiciously; but to say that it is a realiza-
tion of the idea of student self-government,
is to speak absurdly. What the senate
needs is a greater latitude of jurisdiction,
as well as more definiteness of power.

THE SENATE'S WITHDRAWAL.

THE dispute between the senate and the
faculty which resulted in the withdrawal of
the senators by the students in 1894 brought
out in all the student publications of the
college many articles and communications;
all of which were of interest, and many of
them wittily written. Most of these, however, dealt more or less in personalities and
would be out of place in any but a regular

publication of the college. The following communication to the *Student* sums up, without details, one view from an alumnus: " It is fortunate that the present discussion between the faculty and the senate of Amherst college has been made public. We now have before us the several communications that have passed between the two bodies. Both the faculty and the senate agree upon the circumstances involved and the punishment given. A difference of opinion exists as to what body ought to have decreed the penalty. . . After all, it is the welfare of Amherst college that both faculty and senate must keep in mind. Co-operation of the two bodies is the key to their successful work. If the senate did have a cause of grievance against the faculty, it ought to have been stated on other than purely technical grounds. At the same time, this does not excuse the faculty from not entertaining more favorably the senate's request. . . The Amherst senate is already famous within college halls, and for the students to demand or even think of its discontinuance is both hasty and unwise. The senate should hold a most important position in the Amherst idea of self-government. It should be respected by both faculty and students."

From an Almunus Address at Springfield.

THE cutting system and the senate are but milestones along the course of giving the students a larger liberty. The student is on his honor as a gentleman, and may do anything under the sun consistent with that character. The idea is to make the student not only the governed but the governor. The old students thought it meant to break the rules, but given a part in the government they were bound to respect the laws which they themselves had made. The result was the decline and fall of hazing and the almost complete extinction of rowdyism. . . Amherst, that dear old College, so modest in all her pretensions, has shown to the world the possibility and the probability of a self-governing college community. Many colleges have followed her example. Shall that example now fail in the hour of its birth? Shall all that is unique and original in the system be swept away? I hope not. I express the confidence of the alumni in the common sense and wisdom of the senate and faculty to preserve the system, although for years the senate has been the legitimate prey of the *Olio*, the target for the shaft of adverse criticism by some students, and cherish the hope that thè senate will stand as long as Amherst college stands, the queen of the hills "on the banks of the old freshman."

From the Report of the Senior Class.

THE acts of the faculty reduce the senate from the position of a governing body coordinate with the faculty, and acting in a sphere different in kind from that of the faculty, to a subordinate position having such a share in the government of the college as the faculty may see fit to give. Such a subjection of the senate is inconsistent with its independent action. We believe in the Amherst system as it really is, but the subordination of the contract relation and of the senate has undermined that system. Responsibility for student conduct is lifted from the students themselves, where the Amherst system placed it, and assumed, in part at least, by the faculty, who stand once more *in loco parentis* to the students.

It remains, then, for the students to decide if they will acquiesce in the establishment of a new Amherst system and give it their support. Our unanimous opinion is that it would not be for the best interests of the college to do so. The senate is not an end in itself; it exists only as a means for securing good student government, and however much it may have contributed to Amherst's reputation in the past, it should be maintained only so long as it is useful for good student government. We believe that the senate system which would be established by this precedent would be of little usefulness as a governing body and would not secure the respect and co-operation of the students. The question is one which concerns the entire body of undergraduates and should be decided by them.

A NEW "IN LOCO PARENTIS" IDEA.

THERE is a young maid of Amherst,
My grandfather went with her first,
    Soon after my pater,
    And now I myself later,
Will have her if worst comes to worst.

DEDICATION OF THE '89 OLIO.

As the greatest orator of his age has so well and fitly spoken (if we may be permitted to borrow from the store of his eloquence),

We would dedicate this production to Cromwell; but Cromwell was only a soldier. We would dedicate it to Napoleon; but Napoleon made his way to empire over broken oaths and through a sea of blood. We would dedicate it to the Father of his country; but the great Virginian held slaves.

Therefore we dedicate it to the most perfect of all human organizations,

OUR COLLEGE SENATE,

For it never does anything at all.

THE MAIDEN AND HER FRIEND.

(With no especial reference to anybody.)

ONCE on a time there lived a maid,
A maid with noble fame;
Who dwelt within old Amherst's walls,
And she was a beaut., I can tell you, and
everybody was dead stuck on her shape,
and FREEDOM was her name.

Now FREEDOM had a trusty friend—
At least she thought him true—
But subsequent proceedings seemed
To prove pretty conclusively to FREEDOM,
anyway, that you can't most always tell
just what a friend will do.

For when her friend found out that she
Could easily be bossed,
He took her business for his own,
And·pretty soon FREEDOM began to get
onto the fact that her fame, name, and
everything else was most completely
lost.

She found her power all was gone,
Her blessings at an end;
And when she came to figure up,
She allowed that if anybody was responsi-
ble for her loss of dignity and honor, it
was probably that same old friend.

Now, you may read between the lines,
And think you read it well;
But you must do it for yourselves,
And you needn't think we're going to get
ourselves into trouble by explaining the
meaning of this poem, for we aren't;
we're too cooney, and we don't intend
to tell.

AMHERST TYPES AND SCENES.

.

A MATIN IDYL.

WHEN the shades of night are fading,
  And the day begins to dawn,
When rests the tired student,
  With lessons weary and worn,

Then comes upon the morning air
  A hideous pealing knell,
And, with a curse, the student mutters,
  "It is the chapel bell."

Then he rises wearily from bed,
  And hastes his clothes to don;
And ever, as he dresses,
  The cursed bell rings on.

Soon he seizes book and pencil,
  Hat and overcoat as well,
And waltzes off to breakfast,
  To the tune of the chapel bell.

Scarce the doughty steak is tasted,
  Scarce the coffee, sad to tell,

6   67

When, with hasty stroke, "Four minutes
   more,"
Peals out the chapel bell.

Out of the house he rushes,
   With wild and frantic gait,
But three rapid strokes from the tower cry
   out,
   "Too late, old man, too late!"

He slowly turns around and says,
   "What a luckless dog I am."
And then in sad despairing tone,
   "It is the seventeenth, oh ——!"

UBI SUNT, O POCULA!

No more is heard the joke and song
Which did the midnight hours prolong;
No more doth fragrant steam arise
From ham and eggs or chicken pies;
No more we quaff our lemonade
And wink at Kate the waiter maid;
No more we hang up heavy scores,
Since Frank Wood closed to us his doors.

THE ANNUAL PICTURE RUSH.

CHAPTER I.

I⊤ is a beautiful October day. The light is perfect for fixing the beauties of Walker hall and the faces of Amherst's latest accessions on the plate of Pach's camera. Promptly at 2.45 P. M. the sinuous operator ambles to the spot, sets his tripod, limbers his camera, and casts a professional but contemptous glance at the motley crowd on the steps. Some weak attempts at grouping have been made, but the artist's practiced eye quickly notes faults. He is hampered in his re-arrangement by ignorance of names. A good-natured shout greets him, as in mild and trade-beseeching accents he asks, "Will that gentleman with the intelligent-looking face please come forward?" The youth referred to blushingly advances, while the sickly smiles of a few show that they acknowledge the grind on the rest of the class. "Will that very young-looking gentleman sit next the man who is trying to raise a mustache?" brings two startled freshmen into prominence.

The group is completed, and the camera set up. At this juncture a few canes and brush-sticks are stealthily produced from behind some of the stouter men, and accorded prominent places.

CHAPTER II.

Meanwhile a different scene is occurring in the French room. It is nearly time to dismiss the prize division. The commotion of the odious atmosphere made by the vigorous applause at an unusually daring recitation leads someone to open the window. The freshmen and their canes catch his eye. He shouts to the division, who raise the class yell, and bolt without listening to the announcement of " Ten lines in advance."

CHAPTER III.

At the chapel a moment's stop is made, and a hurried consultation ensues. Runners are dispatched to the various tennis courts, and then the main body moves rapidly toward Walker hall. The freshmen sit motionless, for the operator is about to lift the cap ; but how they wish he would hurry, and let them stir ! But he too has seen the advancing mob, and, overcome by terror, quickly takes the advice of a thoughtful sophomore, and removes his apparatus from the cyclone's path.

The sophs break for the center of the group, and the half-dazed freshmen begin to make a few attempts at defense. The more cool and careful step inside the building, deliberately take off coats and hats, and return to the fray; the more impetuous hand their hats to some of the juniors who have begun to gather, and sail in.

Who can describe a lively rush ? There is the pushing, breathless mass in the center, from which some of the stronger and more ambitious are slinging off men, one by one, in their own efforts to get at the cane; the struggling victims in the middle, who would give millions for a free breath; the wounded on the ground; and on the outskirts the squads of more heated partisans, who are anxious to settle the matter by a single knock-down encounter. All must be seen to be appreciated.

Are the whole class engaged? Oh, no ! a few stand hesitant on the steps, wondering if such a struggle can come under Doc's definition of self-defense, or whether it

would break *that contract,* and end their college career should they indulge.

The sophomores get the cane, break it up,
and the recipients start off with their tro-
phies, pursued by the gamy freshmen.
One is downed; and the fight begins again,
but is short lived.   Another cane appears,
and the contestants surge toward the gym.

Thence a well-known figure emerges,
bearing those symbols of authority, the
black book and the fez.   Doc scornfully
looks on until the din subsides, then brings
the book down vigorously on his palm.   A
sharp crack is heard, and a shrill voice
pierces the air, "Young gentlemen, dis-
perse to your rooms !   Juniors, that applies
to you as well !"   The ringing laugh that
follows brings another burst of ire ; and
with "I am not a constable, but you had
better move on, or take the consequences,"
the kindly doctor loses breath, and retires.
The classes, preferring movement to the
consequences, separate, and glide away.

The sophs have exchanged hats, books,
and raiment for glory and inch fragments of
a twenty-five cent cane ; and the freshmen
depart in a battered condition without a
picture.

And where is Pach ? His manly feelings have been outraged. His dignity has suffered the severest insult of all his experience with numerous college classes; but, as his instruments are unhurt, he bottles his wrath, folds up his tent like the Arab, and as silently steals to the train for New York.

THE PLUGGER.

WHO sits from morn till late at night
   His eye upon the page,
And squanders youth and social grace
   To gain in knowledge age ?—
           The plugger.

Who stands so pale before his class
   And pulls a glorious four,
And when exams. send havoc round
   Is first to leave the floor ?—
           The plugger.

Who prides himself upon a key
   Which points to brain alone,
And, culture's pygmy, mounts at last
   The learned commencement throne ?—
           The plugger.

Who makes for life and all its joys
A mere existence do,
And leaves the world no heritage?
'Tis sad to tell, but true—
The plugger.

MINISTERING ANGELS.

THERE are at least five toilers connected with this noble institution whose value is grossly underestimated. I refer to the five daughters of Erin, whose duty it is to effect the weekly sweeping of the dormitories. They are no common drudges; the study of their methods is an inspiring lesson on the amount of interest and even attraction that can be found in the meanest toil merely by absorbing mind and heart in the work. The quantity of ingenuity they display in the apparently simple process of sweeping would do to invent a flying machine.

I will back this statement by proof. For example: They invade a room that is apparently spotless, make a few passes with a broom, and behold a bushel and a half of dirt! Where they get it I cannot tell. Unless we accuse them of familiarity with

the black art, we must admit either that
they brought it with them, or that it was.
there before. In either case their genius is
quite bewildering.

Further illustrations: Having collected
said quantity of dirt, they scatter part of it
on your desk, a larger part in little fuzzy
rolls about the floor, and deposit the rest
behind the piano. The top of the piano,
by the way, they make a repository for
umbrellas, overshoes, base ball bats, and
other equally appropriate articles. They
marshall your rugs in battalion line from
your door to nowhere. They arrange the
Japanese screen so that it will hide the
bookshelves instead of the set-bowl, and
they never fail to swap your desk chair for
your chum's.

These inspiring creatures not only put
thought into their work, but take keen
delight in it, as may be seen from the
following.

If you like to keep your slippers in the
waste basket, where they'll be handy, the
women dump them out with the paper, and
hurry old Charlie downstairs with them.
They do this so that you will have to spend
the rest of the morning in sub-chapel,

rooting through seventeen old rubbish barrels.

In your bedroom they show a fertility of resource that leaves Odysseus a simpleton in comparison. They pile all the clothes they can find on a single chair, and then put something heavy on top of them, so as to muss them as much as possible. They drop your razor strop over behind the bureau, or somewhere where they think you won't find it. They hide one shoe in the bed clothes, and throw the other as far under the bed as the wall will permit, so that you will have to get down on your stomach, and wave madly after it with your cane, and swear.

When they get through with your floor, if they find out that you are studying and want quiet, they detail one of their number to stand at the head of the stairs and slide the brooms, dust pans, mops, etc., down one by one, to the bottom. They do this with great glee, for they know it will make you think things you'll be sorry for afterward.

Sometimes they scrub the hall floor. This is a good deal of work, but they like to do it, for they have discovered an odoriferous washing-powder that discounts any laboratory on the market. It delights them to think that the sickening taint will linger about the halls for a week.

I have just mounted those three weary climbs (what bungling idiot ever named them flights?) of stairs, and have seen two of these calico-vested fairies sitting on the steps and flirting with old Professor Charlie. Innocents! May they be forgiven! As for us—may the saints preserve us!

TO THE PHARISEE.

In our quiet modest way,
To you we'd like to say
That your trick of smiling broadly in the
    class,
When others make mistakes,
Or some very harmless breaks,
Makes you like unto a most consummate ass.
And the way you shake your head,
When anything is said
That does not suit your own precise idea,
When so very oft repeated,
Makes one think you quite conceited,

At least, 'tis so to me it does appear.
   We do not doubt your knowledge,
   You're the pride of all the College,
But this very fault has won you many a
      foe;
   So if you less will do it,
   Or, still better, quite eschew it,
You'll do much to gratify
                        THE OLIO.

THE AMHERST FIRE DEPART-
MENT.

THE small muckers finally succeeded in
rousing up the different members of the fire
brigade, and they gathered slowly about
the post-office steps. After talking for a
short time in subdued tones, one of the
older and more intrepid members mustered
courage to inquire, "Where is it?" No
one appeared to know, and finally two or
three of the more active and headstrong of
the brigade, in spite of the solemn warn-
ings of their elders not to precipitate
matters, started to walk up to college hill
in order to get a view of the surrounding
country, and, possibly, to discover the

whereabouts of the fire, since there seemed to be no way of avoiding the conclusion that there really *was* a fire somewhere. They were spared this trouble, however, by meeting a small boy, who told them the fire was at South Amherst, and they returned to the expectant group at the post-office.

After mature deliberation to decide whether the aforesaid S. B.'s witness should be admitted or not, it was voted by a small majority to get out the engine, and several started for the engine house. After moving a wagon, three ladders, and a worn-out hose carriage, they got the doors open. Here they found that someone had stored a score or two of empty barrels and several dozen dry-goods boxes in front of the engine, but the boys were getting excited now, and in twenty minutes these were all removed and the engine drawn out.

Then ensued a violent discussion as to whether they should draw it by hand or use horses. The advocates of horse-power finally prevailed, and two pairs were sent for. On their arrival, however, it was decided that one pair was sufficient, and the second pair was sent back.

The next difficulty was as to how they should ride, but, at last, having disposed of themselves on various parts of the machine, they started off amid the cheers of the muckers and the admiring gaze of the town fems. Suddenly came a halt. Several members of the department were seen to hold a somewhat hurried consultation. There followed a few moments of suspense. Then it became noised about among the anxious throng who were watching their movements, that the department had forgotten their rubber overcoats.

The excitement was getting tremendous now, and it did not take long to decide that they must have their coats, and to send the ever ready muckers after them. The coats were brought and donned. Then they started again, the town maidens keeping a little way ahead on the sidewalk and looking back with mingled awe and veneration on the advancing cavalcade.

On reaching the foot of college hill, it was decided that all four horses were none too many, and the second pair was sent for. After an extra trip to get splices for the reins, these were attached to the first pair, and again the procession moved on.

When at length the summit of college hill was reached and they actually caught sight of the flames, they gave a yell, in comparison with which the Eighty-four howl became a melodious undertone, and tore down the hill at a marvelous rate of speed., One of the horses gave out on reaching freshman river, but was quickly rolled out of the way and they dashed madly on.

At length the scene of desolation was reached, but they were too late—the fire was out, and after going into the neighboring houses to get warm, they returned home to receive the well-earned plaudits of their fellow-citizens.

It would seem as if the glory thus acquired were sufficient for ordinary mortals, but our gallant fire brigade were soon to add new luster to the crown already won.

It was a calm Sabbath evening, and not a sound disturbed the sacred stillness of the hour, when again there rang out upon the startled air of the cry of fire. The firemen, ever on the alert, gathered in hot haste. They could see all too plainly the bright tongues of flame sweeping upward in the northern skies, until they reached the stars and fired the whole heavens.

Would they get there in time? Well,
they were making desperate efforts and
would probably have succeeded in reaching
the place, had they not become discouraged
when a worthy farmer informed them that
they were running to put out the northern
lights.

One more exploit which capped the cli-
max of their renown and we will close the
thrilling recital.

It was the wild midnight. The tame midnight watchman was off watch and had gone
to bed some time before. The town was
sleeping quietly, all unconscious of the fact
that the wide devastating fire fiend was
doing his disastrous work near by. Happily, one of the gallant sons of Vulcan was
awake. Through a rift in the clouds which
hung over the Pelham mountains he caught
sight of the malignant glow of fire, which
grew brighter and brighter as he gazed.
Pausing only for an instant, he darted
down the stairs and sped through the streets,
raising the terror-fraught cry of *Fire*.

The brave firemen responded with their
wonted alacrity. The engine was manned
and they started on their way, looking
defiantly toward the rapidly increasing

light, when the moon, from above a bank of
clouds, at last shone full upon them with a
serene smile, which seemed to say, "Put
me out if you can," and the story of their
heroic daring is complete.

A MEDITATIVE STUDENT.

A SOLILOQUY.

My thoughts are so profound that their
    profundity is immeasurable,
My mystic meditations deal with themes
    obscure and terrible,
I think and then I meditate, then meditate
    and think,
And then I tell whome'er I meet how much
    I love to think.

I think about myself, and me, and then of
    I, and ego ;
Again about myself, and then about how
    much I know.
I know it all, and even just a little else
    beside ;
And with my knowledge and my thoughts,
    I'm wholly satisfied.

7

Yes, yes, I'm very proud of what I say, and
  think, and know,
And am, and feel, and hear, and see, and
  read and learn ; but oh !
This world's too small for me—I fain would
  soar away,
And tell the men on Mars how much I know
  and think and say.

At length, if I but keep at work, and think
  hard all the time,
I'll have it all thought up; and then, how
  odd and how sublime,
To never rest, but keep at work as hard as
  e'er I can,
And go, and what I have thought up, un-
  think it all again !

THE SPORT'S OFF-DAY.

"Don't talk to me," he said, "I've got
a bad one." It was needless to ask what
his vague statement meant, for he would
have called himself the victim of a bad
"grouch." His more scrupulous room-
mate might have called it a mood, or the

blues, but it all amounted to the same thing. And when I respected his wish and held my peace, he began to speak in a sort of aggressive way, as if daring me to contradict him.

"I don't see what it all amounts to," he said to me, and I knew that more was to follow. "I'm not accomplishing anything. I'm not doing anybody else any good, and I doubt very much if I am profiting by it myself. I am repeating the prodigal son's follies in a way of my own. I'm wasting my father's substance in riotous living. My very mode of life is a systematic and continued deception of the people at home. If I were what my father thought I was I wouldn't be able to put my hat on, and if I fulfilled my mother's expectations nothing short of a halo would do for me. My kid-brother idolizes me, and his one ambition is to be some day the man that he imagines I am now. And she," here he pointed to a photograph on his desk, "she writes that she envies my future, for she knows that my ambition will raise me high above men some day." He stopped speaking, and for a long minute the clock ticks and the crackling of the flames were all that broke the silence. Then he began again. "Yes, I'm deceiving them all shamelessly, but if I told them, it would break their hearts, and if I should change without telling them, they couldn't believe in me any more implicitly than they do now. Two more years in college, lots of time to straighten up in, and—I'm having a good time. Call it wild oats if you want. What do I care?" From quiet regret his voice rose to loud defiance. "Keep your sermons for someone else. I'm going out to-night to eat, drink, and be merry. Don't stay up for me, Tommy."

His room-mate said that it was three o'clock when he came in with thick utterance and unsteady step. The law of compensation had demanded its right, and after his unwonted soberness he had taken pains to lose his sobriety. And the next morning he met me with the old "devil-may-care" expression, which announced, better than words, that earnestness had once more yielded to carelessness.

BEFORE THE FREE DELIVERY.

THE room is not at all prepossessing in appearance. Its bare wooden floor, only a foot above the sidewalk, is invariably soiled with slush, mud, or dust, according to the season of the year. The very door which one encounters on entering is old and dingy and battered, one side being dis-figured by a couple of flaps which look like ill-conceived patches for protection of the holes beneath them. The walls are cov-ered by a motley collection of signs and notices, which only serve to intensify the general air of disregard for ornament or cleanliness. A fly-specked clock adorns one corner, and though this once must have had no mean pretensions to respecta-bility, it now has fallen into the sadly di-lapidated style which pervades the whole place. Not a chair or a bench has ever gained footing within its bare and homely precincts. The view from its spacious windows includes only the roadway, the town pump, and a few brick buildings. Yet there are hours during the day when

this unpretentious—nay, even disagreeable
—apartment is crowded with an eager, expectant gathering.

The explanation of their patient, con-
stant attendance is easy. For all interest
centers about a V-shaped structure which
projects well into the room from the rear
toward the door, lined with a series of little
cells which lend to the whole the appearance of a vast honeycomb. The tiny com-
partments are systematically numbered and
each apparently has its own proprietor.
About these the swarm of busy bees
hovers, each bent on his own cell, finally
turning away content with a white budget
from it, or slowly making off without booty,
showing by his very bearing disappointment that the genius within has not seen
fit to reward his devotions.

Some rarely go away without at least one
of these mysterious white billets, while
some come for days at a time without
receiving any prize at all. But a careful
observer could see that they who oftenest
deposit tribute in a slot at the apex of the
V are most frequently the ones to receive
like tokens. Not seldom the color is lav-
ender, or blue, or pink, these same tints

imparting added value, while those of yellow or bronze exterior are treated with contempt and often cast aside without examination.

Such is this most popular room and such are the proceedings within it. Doubtless the reader has already recognized it. If not, he may see some points of resemblance when at the next mail hour he betakes himself to the Amherst post-office.

THE CONVENTS.

Two convents in a college town,
 Whose fair, sweet nuns, discreet,
March in two dainty throngs each day
 Through the elm-shaded street.

Though guarded by a Saint Bernard
 And by a gallant knight,
Naught of their beauty can be bound:
 It flashes as the light.

Though only from afar can we
 Behold, admire, adore,
Our gracious kindly patron saints
 Be they forevermore!

Fair, gentle saints, inspiring hope,
How they do edify!
Sweet incense on our shrine we burn
To their divinity!

AMHERST REVERIES.

IN AMHERST TOWN.

In Amherst town the blue skies beam
On many a bright and hopeful dream
Of youth, which knows no doubt, no fear,
And thinks of friends and friendships near;
And trusts that men are all they seem.

So this is youth, and youth's bright dream.
It somehow has a brightened gleam
From off the shining sunbeams clear,
    In Amherst town.

And yet a day will come—I deem—
When brightness all away will stream ;
And all the world so dark and drear,
And men so strange; that then I'll hear
They crave again that sunny dream—
    In Amherst Town.

FOUR LIVES.

FROM THE JUNIOR POINT OF VIEW.

STROLLING down the College highway; with
its many ferns and flowers,
Chanced I on four people, trudging on
through all the weary hours.
Each seemed different from the others,
each a different story told,
Which I heard as I was passing, and in
memory still do hold.

SENIOR.

First I met a saddened spinster, old in
years; and worn, and thin,
With a tear-stained face and wrinkled,
pitted with the marks of sin.
She had gone through life, for nothing,
bearing scanty wreaths away,
And I shunned the aged vixen, with her
hideous hair of gray.

JUNIOR.

Then there came a lovely matron rounded
in the prime of life,
Walking on in matchless beauty, carrying
crowns from many a strife.

When she bowed she spoke with sweetness,
and her breath was like the rose,
Like the skies her beauty, sunny grace,
compelling love from foes.

SOPHOMORE.

Next I met a saucy maiden with a dirty, ˙
ugly face,
Shambling on 'mid grievous weeping, with
a walk devoid of grace.
She was overgrown and clumsy, with a
heathen, country air,
And I know not what for rudeness with
this maiden could compare.

FRESHMAN.

Last of all, a funny infant came a-toddling
down the road,
Stubbing 'gainst the stones and squalling in
the latest *à la mode.*
But I rather liked the fellow, with his cute
and childish ways,
For he had the brightest, freshest looks I'd
seen in many days.

Saw I also in the distance, other people
coming on,
But I stopped and did not meet them,—you
may hear of them anon.

In a tavern someone told me, all were Alma
    Mater's kin,
Yet their lives were very different—One
    alone the prize could win.

A REVERIE FROM RHETORIC.

'Twas on an arm in Nungy's room,
    Inclosed by many a penciled square,
    A hideous head with rumpled hair,
Upon an arm in Nungy's room.
Did someone draw that horrid face
    To keep awake to meet his doom;
    Or was the artist's aim to grace
        That old chair arm in Nungy's room?

Perhaps a Goethe traced each line
    Upon that poor defenseless arm,
    And genius' power was the charm
That could create such form divine.
Maybe we'll see a Rubens loom,
    With heaven-sent power and master's
        hand,
    Out from the man who left his brand
On that chair arm in Nungy's room.

Whoe'er he be, where'er he dwell,
    Who drew that frightful image there,
    Long may he live, to have his share

Of blessed life, and live it well.
But may some memory bring him round
  Matured by this world's sun and gloom,
To see what ugly work I found
  On that chair arm in Nungy's room.

AMHERST MISCELLANY.

To order hash or not, that is the question :
Whether 'tis better for man to suffer
The pains and terrors of outrageous hunger,
Or to take hash with all its mysteries,
And by one great gulp to end it.
To eat, perchance to dream, ay, there's the
    rub !
For in that sleep what dreams may come
Of hair, of dogs, of cats, of puppies' tails;
Of shingle nails; of tin tomato-cans;
Of bones; of fishes' tails and fins;
Of skins of apples and potato-rinds.
The choice of hash, or nothing, puzzles the
    will,
And makes us rather bear the hunger that
    we have
Than fly to evils that we know not of.
Thus does this element make cowards of
    us all.

THE EX-SMOKER'S LAMENT.

OFT upon a midnight dreary, while I pon-
  der, weak and weary,
Over many a long and toilsome lesson of
  to-morrow's four,
While I'm nodding, nearly napping, suddenly there comes a tapping,
As of someone gently rapping, rapping on
  his cuspidor.
'Tis my room-mate softly spilling ashes
  from his pipe, for more :
    Only this and nothing more.

At my desk, so slowly working, sit I, with
  no thought of shirking,
Though my will can very little longer
  'gainst this craving war.
How I long to do this rapping, do this soft,
  this gentle tapping,
Filling my old pipe with 'baccy, as so oft in
  days of yore.
Oh, these fetters that restrain me burn into
  my bosom's core :
    For I smoke, ah, nevermore.

Ah, distinctly I remember, and the thought
  is dear and tender,
How I loved to sit and linger over many a
  peaceful smoke.
There I found a way to borrow freedom
  from my every sorrow;
For I'd learned to rout all trouble in wreath-
  ing clouds of smoke.
Often from my dreams I waken, thinking
  that my pledge I've broke:
    But, alas, there's no such hope.

And my pipe is useless lying, all the weed
  within it drying;
In the corner of my desk it's doomed to
  stay for evermore;
While I sit, so vainly trying, all these long-
  ings in me crying
For the smoke of incense, healing to my
  heart so sick and sore;
But my pipe from out that corner, though
  my feelings wage fierce war,
    Can be lifted nevermore.

8

TO THE CONVENT GIRL.

Sᴡᴇᴇᴛ maid, to these bleak hills allured
    To drink thy fill at learning's fount;
Fair being, in whose soul I ween
    Minerva's shrine is paramount;
Do me this grace, sweet lady mine,
    To give my burdened heart relief,
Grant me a hearing, only list
    To my o'erpowering, hopeless grief.

I meet thee oft in aimless stroll
    And view thy passage from afar,
As longingly as sage of old
    E'er watched the rising of his star.
In concert hall I see thee oft,
    And looking, lose all thought of song,
Or muse, or anything except
    The charms that to thyself belong.

Thy presence, too, at vesper-tide
    Enshrines the spot, and all the hour
My homage seeks thy heart alone
    My soul is fast in Cupid's power.
Thus am I tossed with love of thee,
    Thus has my sorrow daily grown,

Now give, I pray thee, beauteous maid,
  Good heed unto that heart of stone,

And see if thou hast not one glance,
  One thought for me. I wait thy word
With anxious heart. Can'st not bestow ˙
  One look on me ? Hast thou not heard ?
˙ Thou can'st not.   Then alas for me !
  What visions now must take their flight.
I blame thee not, but thou hast made
  Of me a most heart-broken wight.

Go on thy course toward wisdom's goal,
  But when at last cute Cupid's bow
Shall pierce thy heart, then, then alone
  Can'st thou my present anguish know.

———

OVER THE NOTCH.

OVER the Notch, 'neath forest-clad height
Rock-strewn, o'er-frowning his path on the
    right,
He wends his swift way to that land of
    delight,
        Over the Notch.

Over the Notch, where the arbutus grows,
Or autumn's bright red midst its pale yel-
    low glows,
Soft breeze from the South in his face
    gently blows,
        Over the Notch.

Over the Notch, to where sweet voices call,
Fair faces glance coyly from window and
    hall,
Or lure him to " Pepper-Box "—best place
    of all—
        Over the Notch.

Over the Notch, in the darkness of night,
The deep, sheer ravine's fearful plunge on
    his right,
Slow and sadly returns he, this love-
    stricken wight,
        Over the Notch.

YE JOLLIE JUNIOR.

ALTHOUGH at ease in outward guise,
    Within his fare he curses.
He can't forget though hard he tries,
    The yawning void his purse is.

AMHERST STORIES.

A DIMPLED PLATONIST.

FERRAND ELIOT was reclining on his window seat. It was a pleasant Saturday afternoon at the beginning of the fall term; here and there a tree had already put on its habit of red or gold, yet the afternoon was not cold, and a gentle breeze fluttered the silken drapery by the open window. Our friend was feeling particularly happy and contented this September day, although he was alone, this being one of his chum's regular days for worship at a certain shrine of Northampton. He held in his hand a sufficiently interesting story; the window seat was comfortable, and it was with a pleasant sense of an ownership of good things that he lay back and lazily surveyed the room before opening the volume. His eyes wandered over the familiar things— the regulation sets of foils, masks, and boxing-gloves, the college bric-a-brac, the "Ladies' Cloak Room" and "Reserved," signs of freshman year; the patriotic purple

and white banner, and several water-color
sketches, Ferrand's own work; the mantel
with its array of pipes, and a few medals
won at Worcester or in the heavy gym.
All these things his eyes surveyed with
an expression of great content, until they
came to rest upon the most charming thing
in the room—the photograph of a young
girl. Then, strangely enough, the placid
expression changed to one of contending
admiration, pity, and disgust. "Why
should Frank make such a fool of himself?"
he asked the ceiling—"and for her to throw
herself away like that!" Ferrand Eliot
was a well-born and well-bred Virginian,
manly, broad-shouldered, blue-eyed; a type
which cannot be surpassed anywhere. The
"sand" and skill which he exhibited on
the football eleven, where he played right
guard, together with his accurate scholarship in the classroom, showed that his
muscle and the fiber of his brain were
equally tough. He was a man whom everyone trusted. But there was a screw loose,
as the fellows said.

, In matters of sentiment Ferrand Eliot
was a Platonist. He thought it not only
nonsense, but downright suicide, for two

young people to fall in love with each other. "Why won't they be sensible?" he would exclaim. "Look about and see all the unhappiness lovers bring on each other and the rest of the world. It could be avoided so easily. What an absurdity to say that a young man and a young woman cannot be the closest friends, without degenerating into the sickly sentimental style of inter- course!" He had lived a score of years, and had known many women intimately, but his platonic heart was still untouched by any unplatonic passion.

On the other hand, his chum, Frank Hanway, held exactly opposite views. He claimed that he had always been in love, as has every other man, acknowledge it or not. "We all have our ideals," he would say, "and sooner or later every man will find attributes of his ideal centered in some woman." And so, of course, they had many long and amusing discussions on these interesting topics. There was something fascinating in Hanway's way of putting things which attracted his chum, while the latter's manly sincerity Frank felt to be worthy of respect. Now, Hanway had already found his ideal in the subject of the admired, pitied, and obnoxious photograph, the fascinating Miss Alger of Smith college. So he had lost no time in using man's privilege by telling Miss Alger that he had always loved her, although until a fortnight previous to the declaration they had been utter strangers.   Miss Alger, while her confession may have been less striking, was none the less in love with Frank Hanway. To most of their friends it seemed a perfect match.   Not so to Ferrand; he could not be reconciled to such an abnormal state of things.   Miss Alger was a pretty girl. Frank was a thorough good fellow.   But the combination was intolerably absurd. The window seat was no longer comfortable. He frowned, fidgeted, and finally arose, pulled on his cap, and sought the companionship of his "Columbia," of whose platonic friendship he felt secure.   But why did he take the road to Northampton ?

At Northampton he turned to the left, crossed the meadows, ferried the Connecticut at Hockanum, and followed the winding river toward South Hadley. The beauty of the quiet river; of the meadows dotted over with white houses and tobacco barns; of Northampton with it churches and colleges like pretty mosaics set in the emerald of wonderful elms; of the little rifts and puffs of smoke from furnaces and creeping engines so far away, there was charm enough in all this to cause Ferrand to slacken his speed. Too great haste amid such surrounding loveliness would have been an impertinence, if not a sacrilege. He had ascended the long hill which rises abruptly out of the river, and turned his head as he began the descent to get a last glimpse of the quiet valley.

There must have been some sort of misfit in the road, for he turned a somersault in the air and several on the ground, and saw stars for some moments. Among the stars he perceived a straw sailor-hat, a tennis-dress, and a frightened face. In due time the stars retired to their proper orbits, but the other articles considerately stayed, to resolve themselves into a very presentable young lady.

"Can I help you?" said the young lady, regarding apprehensively a certain part of Ferrand's head which bulged ominously.

"Thank you, very much," he said, getting slowly to his feet, and having sufficient

presence of mind to touch his cap. "I
shall do very well, I think."

"Then I may smile just a little?" she
asked. "I'm not ill-natured, but there is
such a funny side to an accident of that
sort!"

She stood by the roadside dimpling
softly, her brown hair blown backward.
Ferrand began to be interested. It was
certainly a strange manner for a young
girl to use toward a stranger. Yet it
was not familiar. In the presence of a
"header," according to Ferrand's experience, most young ladies would choose
to scream or faint or giggle. Here was
one who had promptly offered her aid, but
evidently had no uncalled-for sentimental
sympathy to deal out, even to such a good-
looking young gentleman as Ferrand felt
himself to be. To be sure there was a
smirch of the roadway across his face, and
his clothes were shockingly begrimed, but
even then! He rid himself impatiently of
a little of the dirt, and collected his cap
and his bicycle before turning to say a few
decent phrases in his best ladies' manner.
She was seated further back from the road,
sketching quietly, with a little preoccupied

knot in her brow and her head on one side. Ferrand took off the rescued cap.

"You were very kind to try to help me, and I forgive the smile," he said. It was quite as unconventional a remark as hers had been, he thought. She looked up at him.

"I am really glad you weren't hurt seriously, Mr. Ferrand Eliot," she said.

This explained the whole thing. It was someone he had met and forgotten; and yet Ferrand did not forget easily.

She was quick to notice the embarrassed, remembering expression on his face.

"No, you needn't try. You have never met me anywhere, and yet I know you quite well, Mr. Ferrand Eliot," she said.

"I give it up," said Ferrand, laughing. He had no doubt that this self-possessed young lady would explain in her own good time. In the meanwhile there was no hurry. But she laid down her sketchbook.

"In the first place," she said, "you are a chum of a certain Amherst man named Mr. Frank Hanway, aren't you?"

"Yes," said Ferrand, "but——"

"In the second place, Mr. Frank Hanway is engaged, I believe they call it, to a

certain Smith girl called Miss Alger, isn't
he ? "

"Why, yes," said Ferrand, "but
how——"

"In the third place, I am the room-
mate of this Miss Alger, who is engaged
to the man who lives with the man whose
name is Ferrand Eliot. Now do you
see ?"

"Oh, yes," cried Ferrand, "and you are
Miss——" Here he stopped and thought
hopelessly.

"Ah," she said, dimpling again, "you
aren't so well informed about me as I am
about you. Allow me to introduce myself
in a shockingly irregular manner as Miss
Helen Prescott, at your service, sir."
With this she bowed meekly.

"Of course," said Ferrand. "How
stupid ! But that doesn't explain how you
recognized me."

"Oh, you were pointed out to me at
the first football game, so the mystery is
all gone."

"I wonder if you have your chum's interests at heart as much as I have mine,"
said Ferrand. "If you have, you have a
grudge against Frank Hanway."

"Yes, indeed, I have!" she cried. "Do you know, you men are a bit provoking with your brag about stanchness, fidelity, and all the other solid virtues which women are supposed not to possess. As if women couldn't be as good friends as men!"

"I think you are right," he asserted, "and I only wish all women were as sensible as you; but what is still more provoking to me, is the generally accepted idea that a man and a woman—you and I, for instance—can't be together and enjoy each other's companionship without going through the absurd process of falling in love. Now, there are Frank and Miss Alger—but it's of no use to argue with Frank," and Ferrand turned his brown head impatiently.

"And Margaret is quite as obstinate," said Miss Prescott gloomily. "Isn't it a pity!" This was certainly a very unusual girl. She was pretty, but of course that was a secondary matter, thought Ferrand. It was her frankness and good sense that were so attractive. He followed a sudden impulse.

"Miss Prescott," he said, "what do you say to our demonstrating to these beloved

idiots the strength of our position? I like
you, at all events——"

"And I like you, Mr. Eliot," said Helen
Prescott. "And here is my hand to clinch
the bargain. We must save those children!
And now, to show that you are in earnest,
I wish you would go away at once! The
other girls left me here to do some sketching, and it is time for them to return with
the carriage. I should like to have you
meet them, but it might be rather unpleasant for you, looking as you do, you know—
and we have met in such a singular way.
And, if.you should come to the Hubbard
house with Mr. Hanway some time I
should be very pleased to *meet* you." A
dimple and a courtesy, and Ferrand found
himself dismissed.

"The fact of our first meeting for con-
spiracy is to be kept in the dark, then," he
reflected, as he rode slowly toward the
ferry, "or is it merely a feminine tribute
to the goddess Grundy?" So it happened
that he told Frank about the accident, without mentioning its other than material consequences. He felt a little guilty, but it
was a consolation that his guilt was shared.

It came to pass a week later that, as they

were walking down from chapel together,
Ferrand said :

" I suppose you are off to Hamp, as
usual, this evening, to see the fair one ? "

" Yes," said Frank, shrugging his
shoulders, and expecting to hear the usual
tirade about "sentimental bosh," and so
forth.

" Well," said Ferrand, " I think I'll come
with you and hear the turtledove coo, if
you don't mind."

Whereat Frank wondered greatly, for
hitherto his efforts at bringing together his
chum and his sweetheart had been frus-
trated by a true Virginian obstinacy.

That evening Ferrand was duly presented
to Miss Alger.

" Not so bad," thought Ferrand; " she
doesn't look like a maniac. But then the
way she looks at Frank! And they would
have been quite as comfortable if they
hadn't shaken hands for quite five minutes. '

They had spoken the introductory com-
monplaces, when in came the demure Miss
Prescott, who expressed herself as delighted
to *meet* Mr. Eliot. But there was a stray
dimple for Ferrand alone—when the turtle-
doves had drawn aside with an uncon-

9

sciously relieved expression—which showed
that she had not forgotten their bargain.

We need not say how often during the
following winter Ferrand spent his evenings
in Northampton, nor how many letters with
double postage passed and repassed the
long bridge; there were so many things to
be talked over with reference to the refor-
mation of the lovers.   So far, indeed, from
there being any immediate gratifying results in the behavior of the lovers, conse-
quent to the Platonic example so studiously
set for them, they seemed to be getting more
and more incurable.   But everything does
not come to pass in a day, and the two con-
spirators labored on.

So senior year sped by, and the commencement day partings drew near, and
the evening came when Frank and Ferrand
must make their last visit upon the Hubbard house piazza.   Not that Frank cared
a whit; he was all in the future; the Hubbard house had been to him a rather
inconvenient place of tryst.   But to Ferrand it was a melancholy time.   To keep
alive an intellectual friendship across a con-
tinent is no easy matter, in spite of the
graphs and phones of this privileged age.

He found himself looking with envy upon his chum, who was not to know the pangs of intellectual separation. Frank had some errands to do, and Ferrand found Miss Prescott alone. They shook hands in their usual business-like way. But they did not succeed in being very talkative.

"I'm afraid all our efforts have been a vanity, after all," she said; "we have had a great deal of trouble for nothing, haven't we?" She was sitting with her back to the light, and he could see her dimpled cheek in profile.

"For nothing?" he said mechanically. She turned slightly, so that he saw a little helpless quiver of her under-lip. He rose from his chair, throwing out his arm as if to cast off some weight. Then he came before her, raised her gently to him, and looked long and lingeringly into her face. It was not very long after this that the two foolish lovers came into the room, and were naturally surprised. The fellow-philosophers looked, to tell the truth, a little sheepish.

"This isn't a very good example——" began Helen.

"The simple truth of the whole matter

is," said Ferrand, calmly but with unction, "that Plato was an old fool!"

But I doubt if Plato could have withstood those dimples.

LE ROY PHILLIPS, '92.

A POLITICAL DEAL.

REGINALD THOMPSON's face was clouded as he lounged on the window-seat, and even the smoke-wreaths from his pipe floated away with an air of dreariness.

Reginald was only a sophomore, yet he was taking a farewell look at the books, the pictures, and the knickknacks in his room. In a short time he was to be expelled from college.

A few evenings before, a freshman had been suddenly seized while strolling about the campus, and had been blindfolded before he could catch more than a glimpse of his assailants. He had been led away and hazed. In the midst of the fun his tormentors were interrupted by the approach of a watchman. They fled around a corner, only to encounter another man. But he was hurrying to catch a train and had no time to trouble himself about the disturbance. So the fugitives passed him without interference, and there was no one to tell who they were unless the victim himself had some idea. And, in fact, the latter had stated most positively that one of his tormentors had been Reginald Thompson; that he had not only recognized Thompson's voice, but had even caught a glimpse of him. The accused denied the charge in vain; only his most intimate friends would believe him, for he had not been in his room on that evening, and no one could say where he had been.

The laws of the college required that hazing be punished with expulsion; but first, the student must come before the college senate, and without the sanction of this body no action could be taken.

A meeting of the senate had therefore been called by the president, but had been postponed because one of the sophomore members had not yet been elected.

Thompson's chum and room-mate, William MacMaster, was the president of the sophomore class, and was using his influence to the utmost to help his friend. Reginald knew this, and his face brightened considerably when MacMaster burst in upon his meditations on the window seat.

"Hello, Reggie !" he cried; "stop your scowling now, old man, and cheer up, I have some good news."

"Well, Bill, what is it?" asked Reginald, with a smile that was almost gloomy.

"The election will be to-morrow and Townsend is going to run for senatorship," began the other as he sat down and shoved both his hands into his pockets. "All of our crowd, of course, will vote for him, and I made a deal with the Theta Epsilons, so that they will be in for him too."

"It is awfully kind of you, Bill, to take so much trouble for me."

"Come now, you had better keep your thanks until you are well out of this scrape. I have seen all the senators and they seem to be equally divided for and against you, so that Townsend's election is absolutely necessary."

"Who else will run for senator?" asked Reggie.

"Oh, I nearly forgot to tell you that. The other side will vote for Borden."

"That's bad news. I always hated that man, and I guess he was not over fond of me. He is a low, mean sort of a fellow."

"Yes, I know," answered MacMaster, "and he has a strong pull with the ouden's. But he won't stand the ghost of a show. Now I must go and canvass some more

votes. So I'll see you later." And with
this assurance MacMaster left his friend to
relight his pipe.

The next day came and with it the sophomore election. The chapel was filled with
the members of the class, but there was not
the usual laughing and bluffing. The boys
felt the importance of the meeting. They
knew the effect that their votes would have
on Reggie's happiness, and, though he was
well liked, all were indignant at the hazing
that had been done; the sentiment of the
class was against it, and the boys had decided to vote as they believed their class-
mate deserved.

As Bill MacMaster entered the room arm
in arm with Townsend, he was greeted with
a cheer. But he took little notice of the
greeting, and sat down apparently in anxious
thought. A little later, a short, thick-set
man entered the room amidst applause almost as loud as that which had greeted
MacMaster and Townsend. In acknowl-
edgement of the applause he bowed his
large head with its matted covering of
black, curly hair, and smiled with a look of
superiority.

It was Alvan Borden, the other candidate.

His coarse features were full of character, and his small, dark eyes twinkled from shaft-like depths. One could see at first sight the power and ability of the man; yet it seemed ability more for the bad than for the good.

Since he had thought it would be awkward, if not indelicate, Thompson did not come to the meeting.

When the room was well filled, MacMaster arose and called the meeting to order, and they proceeded to the election of the senator.

Besides Townsend and Borden there was one other nominee. The informal ballot was collected, and showed forty-six votes for Townsend, for Borden thirty-seven, and a few for the third man. This result made MacMaster feel assured, as he called gayly for the second ballot, that Townsend would be elected. But then the votes were again collected, and the secretary read, "Townsend has forty-seven votes, and Borden fifty. Mr. Borden is elected."

This time MacMaster looked around helplessly. He felt that his chum's last chance was gone. He had not expected defeat, and it was some time before his feelings allowed him to ask: " Is there any further business ? "

The same evening the meeting of the senate was held, and both Reginald and the victim of the hazing appeared.

Again the freshman told the story of the hazing, and accused Reginald of being one of his tormentors, and again the sophomore denied the charge, but acknowledged that he had no proof. "Very well," said the president, who presided over the meeting; "if you have nothing else to say in your defense, you may withdraw to the next room and await the decision of the senate." Reginald went out and threw himself down on one of the hard wooden benches. He knew too well what the decision would be, for since Borden had been elected senator he had given up even the faintest hope. He was younger and more sensitive than most of his fellows. Some men in his position would have shown boastful indifference which they would have mistaken for manliness. But not so Reginald; he dreaded the results and longed for some proofs of his innocence. Thoughts of the disgrace and of his father's disappointment jostled through his brain. Why did not those who had really done the deed acknowledge it and free him from the punishment? Then his thoughts wandered to facing the decision, but a few moments off, and he determined to meet it as firmly as possible. He would be ashamed to show any weakness. So he mustered up his courage and waited patiently. It was only a few minutes later that he heard the latch behind him turn, and looking around he saw Borden's massive, ugly head poked through the half-opened door.

"The president sent me to summon the culprit to reappear before the meeting," said the senator jeeringly. "Will you kindly follow?"

Reginald bit his lips and followed, but his resolve not to flinch was strong, and he stood before the president's desk without wavering.

Then the president said: "Reginald Thompson, the senate has decided that on account of your actions against the freshman whom you hazed you are unworthy to be any longer a member of this college. Hereafter you will attend none of the recitations or exercises."

Reginald turned and was just walking

toward the door when it flew open, and in rushed MacMaster, followed by another man. The class president was excited and he evidently brought news. His eyes were flashing, his cheeks were reddened with running, and a smile of exultation touched his lips. Then, remembering the decorum proper before the president, he checked himself and said, as calmly as his excitement would allow, "Mr. President, excuse my interruption; I hope that you have not yet voted upon this matter, for I have found a witness."

"I am very glad to hear it," replied the president, "for we want all possible light. What has the witness to say? It is not too late, if it is anything of importance."

The newcomer stepped forward and, after a moment's hesitation, addressed the president: "As I was hurrying to catch a train on last Friday evening I heard the watchman shouting, 'Stop those fellows! Stop them!' and at the same time two college men ran past me at full speed. I had only just time enough to catch my train, so, without taking much notice of the trouble, I hurried on. To-day, when I returned from my trip, I found the whole

college talking about some hazing that had
been done on the evening when I left town;
I found that Thompson of the sophomore
class had been accused of being one of the
culprits, and that as such he was to be expelled from college. I asked for particu-
lars, and it was proved to me that the two
men who ran past me as I was going to my
train last week were the very ones who had
done the hazing. Reginald Thompson,
sir,—" the last sentence was said very deliberately,—" Reginald Thompson was not
one of these two."

The whole room had been perfectly quiet
while the testimony was being given, and
when it was finished there was a look of
relief upon the faces of all, with one exception. The president smiled with satis-
faction, for he had been troubled through-
out the affair by the steady denial of the
supposed culprit; and most of the senators
shared his feelings, even those who had
voted against Thompson. Alvan Borden
alone did not feel the universal pleasure.
If one had watched him while the witness
had been speaking, one would have seen
how those deep-sunken eyes flashed with
hate, and how he longed to pounce like

a tiger upon the witness and stop his testimony. But no one noticed him, and when the witness had finished and all eyes turned toward the president, the senator's, too, followed in forced composure.

Then the president, remembering his duty, asked of the witness: "Since Mr. Thompson was not one of the two men whom you met, can you tell us who they were ?"

"One of them I refuse to name," was the reply, "for the punishment of the other will be enough for a precedent. He was Mr. Borden."

If the meeting had been surprised when Reginald had been proved not guilty, it was still more so at this sudden accusation of the real culprit, and all looked toward Borden, expecting on his part at least a denial of the allegation. But they were disappointed, for, with a look of dogged indifference, he waited silently until the president had asked: "Do you acknowledge these things, Mr. Borden ?"

Then indeed his sullen eyes flashed in their deep sockets, and, since he saw that denial was useless, he answered, "I do."

ALFRED ROELKER, Jr., '95.

SAWYER'S HOLIDAY.

WHEN we asked Sawyer to go with us for a "quiet little time" on Mountain Day he refused. It is unnecessary to say that we were greatly surprised. For heretofore Sawyer had been the most anxious of us all to go off for a celebration; it had always been Sawyer who had taken the leading part at such times—and Sawyer had always felt the worst the next day.

So when he refused—and his language was not uncertain—we knew there must be some strong reason for his decision. "Going somewhere else?" asked Tomkins. "No; got to stay right here in Amherst all day." "Hang the money; your credit is still good with me," said Badger. "'Taint money, Badge, old boy. Thanks very much,—no, I don't mind borrowing a little more,—but I have to be here—fact is, fellows, I am going to work all day."

To such a declaration as that from Sawyer we could make no immediate reply. It was as though the sun should rise over Northampton some morning and pass across the heavens eastward, settling behind the Pelham hills at night, in which case we feel very sure language would fail to express our consternation. And thus we were at first dumfounded at Sawyer's words.

It was natural, however, that we should all try to offer some explanation for Sawyer's conduct. "Crazy," said Badger. "Looking for a three," disdainfully remarked Tomkins. "Getting pious, more likely," said I. "No, it isn't any of those things, fellows. I'll tell you; you see, here it is senior year and I have not done any work since winter term sophomore year. I have a lot of things to pass off, and I don't want to leave them all till senior vacation—they might interfere with class-supper. So I'm going to stay home Mountain Day and get some of them up. I think there are seven in all, and I guess I can nail four of of them on that day."

This explanation from Sawyer we all considered insufficient.

"Why, I've got six myself, old man," said Tomkins, "and I'm going to leave them till some Sunday next term. Besides it's our last Mountain Day, Jack, and we ought to celebrate."

But it was all of no use, and so we went
without Sawyer, missing him every moment
of the day and half wishing we had stayed
at hóme.

And this is the way Sawyer kept Mountain Day.

He set his alarm clock at five-thirty, so
that he could do his mathematics before
breakfast. Then during the forenoon he
was going to write nine essays for the
rhetoric department—essays for which he
had no time when they were due. That
would leave the afternoon for fall term's
physics, and in the evening he could easily
read over a term's German. It all seemed
very easy, and I am convinced that Sawyer
really thought he would enjoy the day as
much as though he went with us.

When the alarm went off at half-past five
Sawyer thought of his resolutions and got
right up. It was an entirely new experience for him to do any work before breakfast, but after a few unnecessary prelimi-
naries, which included a walk around the
common, he considered himself ready for
work. By breakfast time he had reviewed a
quarter of the mathematics and was tired,
but encouraged. After breakfast he started

10

directly for his room, but, remembering
that he expected a letter, he changed his
mind and went to the post-office. As he
was coming away from the office he met
Jones, who asked him to have a game of
billiards. Jones was the man who had
beaten him twice within a week; Sawyer
had been waiting for a chance to play with
him again, for he disliked to remember an
unavenged defeat from so unpopular a man
as Jones. But it was out of the question
for him to play then; so he answered,
"Sorry, but I am very busy to-day, Jones—
some other time."

Jones looked rather surprised and smiled
a little. Sawyer recognized the weakness
of his excuse, and so, as Jones was turning
away, he ran over the situation in his own
mind. "The math. is practically done; I
can do those essays in three hours, and
that will leave plenty of time for the
German. Besides, I've studied three
hours already this morning and am tired.
I guess a little recreation will clear up my
head—I don't want to get sick studying."
So he called to Jones and said he did have
time, after all. This seemed more satis-
factory to Jones, and so they went up to

the hotel. The result of it was that Jones won the first two games, and only by the most careful kind of play did Sawyer get the next three. When they'had finished it was eleven o'clock, and Sawyer hurried to his room to begin on the rhetoric. At his room he found the morning paper and he smoked a pipe over that, saying to himself, "A fellow can't afford to get behind on the questions of the day—especially just before election."

By dinner time he had written one of those nine essays, and had decided the theme of another one. He and Wilkins were the only ones at dinner,—everyone else was observing the day.

"What 've you been doing this morning, Sawyer?—haven't seen you at all," said Wilkins.

"No, I've been working ever since five o'clock this morning; I'm tired as the deuce, too. I never knew before how much a fellow could do in a day; I've practically made up a term's math. and a term's rhetoric."

"Oh, yes; when a fellow applies himself he can do a lot of work in a few hours. Going away this afternoon?"

" No; going to finish up the day as I've begun it."

After dinner Sawyer went directly to his room and filled his pipe. He reviewed the situation again : "I˙can finish the essays in another hour, and get the German out before supper. Then what will I do this evening? Oh! yes, physics. That will take fully two hours. Guess I ought to have a little nap—can work better after it."

So he got onto the window-seat and took a nap which lasted till after three. He was wakened by a rap at the door which proved to be by a boy with a special delivery letter. The letter bore the postmark Northampton, and was as follows :

" MY DEAR MR. SAWYER :

" My roommate was agreeably surprised this noon to receive a telegram from her friend Mr. Blewes of Yale, saying that he would call this afternoon. As it is impossible for us to get a team, we are going to have a little tea this afternoon about five, and we want you to make the fourth one. You can readily see that the tea will be a complete failure without you—for three is a very ugly number. So please come—if you don't I'll never—— I expect you without fail.

"As ever, most cordially yours,
"GRACE TALMADGE.
"Smith College, Thursday noon."

Of course Sawyer's first thought was to go over. Then he remembered that he had a little work to do, and the result was a burst of profanity which was by no means mild. But it was far from natural that anything should stand in Sawyer's way when this particular young lady was concerned. And he reasoned it all out this way : "I've done the math. and rhetoric; there was really only one thing I didn't understand in that physics, and I can get that up after I get back to-night. It will be easy to bluff the German. So I have already done practically everything I had planned for to-day. Besides, my head aches and I feel a little feverish—staying in doors too much, I guess. That is a mighty pleasant note from Grace—er—from Miss Talmadge, I mean. I'll have to drive over, won't I ? Wonder if I'd better take up some flowers— very informally; white roses I guess—no, pink; those go better with her complexion.

It's lucky I stayed home to-day. Glad I did all my work this forenoon—it pays not to put things off."

As he was thinking the situation over to himself in this way he had already begun to dress, meantime whistling the classic which tells of O'Grady's swimming abilities.

Sawyer's toilet was unusually elaborate that afternoon, but in due course of time he might have been seen going toward the livery stable. Although it was Mountain Day he was able to get a team, by means of which one hour later he was in Northampton. The walk up Elm Street was not as interesting as usual, because there were fewer maidens to watch him from behind half-opened shutters or partly drawn curtains. But the end in view made the walk even under these depressing conditions far from unpleasant. They were waiting for him and She was radiant. The chaperon was not bad—the best thing about her (so Sawyer thought) was that she was called out soon after he arrived and that she came back only in time to say good-night, two hours later. Of course they were all glad he came; Blewes and the roommate because now Miss Talmadge

would not be in their way, and Miss Talmadge herself because she was no longer
an odd one. She told Sawyer how she had
worried lest he should not come, and how
awfully provoking it would have been ;—
all of which Sawyer considered personal.
Then he told her how he had worked all
day long from five o'clock till the time he
received her note, a little after four, and
how he had hurried to get over in time; all
of which Miss Talmadge said was awfully
hard luck. Then Sawyer went on to say
that he was glad it was senior year, as he
was getting very tired with all the work he
had on hand, and he was anxious to get
into business. And Miss Talmadge agreed
that he looked tired and that doubtless a
change would do him a great deal of good.

Blewes and the roommate seemed to be
very well acquainted, and for the most part
they confined their conversation to themselves. The time went very swiftly because
pleasantly, until Sawyer heard the clock
strike six. Then he made a movement to
go, saying that he had some work for the
evening, but the girls would not listen to
such an excuse. After that Sawyer told
her that he and some friends were going to

give a german in a few weeks and he would like to have her attend. Of course she blushed and thanked him, saying that he was very kind, and that if he was sure he wanted her she thought perhaps she could arrange it. And Sawyer said of course she was the one he wanted and that he should have absolutely no pleasure if she did not go. So she promised and they shook hands on it, prolonging the handshake a few moments till Blewes turned to ask Sawyer about Amherst's football team.

But at last it was time to go, as Blewes had to catch a train. Sawyer told the chaperon (who had come in a little while before) that they had missed her greatly, and that they were sorry she had been called away. Then he reminded Miss Talmadge of her promise and they said goodnight all around. Sawyer and Blewes walked down town together and parted by the post-office. Sawyer felt too well satisfied with the world in general and with himself and Miss Talmadge in particular to go home and to work again. He reasoned that after such a jolly time as he had just been having a little celebration was necessary. So he hunted up some of the boys (it was not a difficult task, for he knew where to search for them) and the evening passed very quickly. It was twelve instead of eight o'clock when Sawyer got to his room. By that time he had forgotten all about the work he had planned, and so he went to bed.

The next day Sawyer asked us if we had a good time. We said that of course we did. Whereat he replied, "I'm mighty sorry I couldn't be with you, boys, but still I'm glad I stayed at home, for you see I made up practically four conditions, and now I'm sure of my diploma."

And ever since that day Sawyer has borne witness to the theory that the only condition necessary to the accomplishment of hard work is conscientious application.

CHAS. AMOS ANDREWS, '95.